CREEPER INVASION

CREEPER INVASION

AN UNOFFICIAL MINETRAPPED ADVENTURE, #5

Winter Morgan

Sky Pony Press
New York

Copyright © 2016 by Hollan Publishing, Inc.

Minecraft® is a registered trademark of Notch Development AB.

The Minecraft game is copyright © Mojang AB.

Sky Pony Press books may be purchased in bulk at special discounts for sales
promotion, corporate gifts, fund-raising, or educational purposes. Special
editions can also be created to specifications. For details, contact the Special
Sales Department, Sky Pony Press, 307 West 36th Street, 11th Floor,
New York, NY 10018 or info@skyhorsepublishing.com.

Sky Pony® is a registered trademark of Skyhorse Publishing, Inc.®,
a Delaware corporation.

Minecraft® is a registered trademark of Notch Development AB.
The Minecraft game is copyright © Mojang AB.

Visit our website at www.skyponypress.com.

10 9 8 7 6 5 4 3 2 1

Library of Congress Cataloging-in-Publication Data is available on file.

Cover design by Brian Peterson
Cover photo by Megan Miller

Print ISBN: 978-1-5107-0601-9
Ebook ISBN: 978-1-5107-0611-8

Printed in Canada

TABLE OF CONTENTS

CREEPER INVASION

1
LISIMI LAND

Lily looked down from atop the Ferris wheel and stared at Lisimi Land. She sat next to Simon and remarked, "I can't believe we've actually finished Lisimi Land. It's amazing!"

"That's what happens when people work together. You're right. Lisimi Land is terrific. It's such a super, awesome amusement park." Simon smiled.

Lisimi Land was bustling. All of the townspeople were spending the afternoon enjoying the many thrill rides that filled the park. There was a long line for the roller coaster and another for the fun house.

"I think I've been on every ride." Lily scanned the park from the Ferris wheel.

Simon looked out as the Ferris wheel went around. "I haven't been in the fun house yet. Would you like to go again?"

Lily thought about the fun house. She liked it, but there were parts of the fun house that bothered her. The fun house gave out a texture pack that made everything slanted. She paused; she didn't want to disappoint Simon, but she really didn't want to go through the fun house again. "Would you mind if I don't go to the fun house with you?"

"Why?" Simon was shocked.

"It's not for me. I find it slightly scary," Lily confessed.

"Scary?" Simon questioned. "We're stuck on a Minecraft server where we have battled every hostile mob in the Overworld, Nether, and the End, and you're scared of the fun house. That's funny, Lily."

"It's not funny." Lily was angry. "I was being honest with you. I didn't enjoy it."

Simon felt badly. "I'm sorry, Lily. I didn't mean to upset you."

"It's okay," Lily said. "I just don't want to be made fun of for admitting I'm afraid."

Simon smiled. "Remember how witches used to terrify you? And now you're not bothered by them?"

"They still bother me, but I'm not paralyzed by fear anymore. I've destroyed enough witches to know that I'll be fine if one of them tries to attack me," explained Lily.

The Ferris wheel ride was over. Before they stepped off the ride, Simon suggested going for another ride on the Ferris wheel, but Lily didn't want to. "Where do you want to go next?" asked Simon.

"I think you're right. It's very silly of me to be afraid of the fun house. I'm going to try going through it again."

"You don't have to do that. We can go on something else," Simon suggested. "How about the waterslide? Or the new roller coaster? Or bumper cars?"

All of Simon's ideas sounded great, but Lily wanted to conquer her fears. She wanted to go through the fun house again. "I really want to go in the fun house. It's the only part of the park that you haven't been in and I think you'll like it."

As Simon and Lily walked toward the fun house, they spotted Mr. Anarchy rushing toward them. He looked upset.

"Mr. Anarchy," Lily asked, "are you okay?"

Mr. Anarchy caught his breath. "No, something awful has happened. I was experimenting on a way to get off the server and I was with Warren. I think I accidently zapped him off the server."

"That's great news!" Lily exclaimed. "How did you do it? Now we can all leave."

"I'm not certain I zapped him off. I could have accidentally erased him from existence. I'm not sure." Mr. Anarchy spoke fast as his eyes welled with tears.

"What are you talking about?" Lily asked. "You have to take a deep breath and speak slowly. I want you to explain everything that happened."

Before Mr. Anarchy had a chance to reply, Juan the Butcher approached them. "Something is very wrong. I just saw a group of six creepers in the center of the town."

"What? That sounds like someone has spawned them," Lily cried out. "That could only be the work of a griefer."

Mr. Anarchy didn't want to hear about the creeper invasion. He was too upset over Warren's disappearance. "We can destroy the creepers, but we have bigger problems."

"What could be more important than a creeper invasion?" Juan the Butcher questioned.

"Warren's disappearance is more important." Mr. Anarchy took a deep breath as he told Juan what happened to Warren. "We were using command blocks to summon lightning that might zap us back to the real world when Warren disappeared. There wasn't a lightning bolt or anything. He simply vanished."

"How?" Lily questioned.

"I don't know," replied Mr. Anarchy.

Juan paused. "Do you think the creeper invasion and Warren's disappearance might be related?"

The gang wondered if this could be the case. Lily replied, "If that's true, we might have to battle a griefer."

"Has anyone checked on Pablo, Ronan, and Matthew?" asked Simon.

"I stopped by the prison on my way here and the guards were out front. It looked like everything was fine," said Mr. Anarchy.

"We have to get to the bottom of Warren's disappearance," Simon said.

"And we have to stop the creepers!" Juan warned them, as he pointed out several creepers silently floating through the gates of Lisimi Land.

Lily grabbed her bow and arrow from her inventory and shot an arrow at a creeper.

Kaboom!

Simon and Mr. Anarchy also aimed their bows at the creepers, destroying the fiery mob with their arrows.

Ilana ran over to them. "What's happening? Why are there so many creepers in Lisimi Land?"

"I don't know, but we're going to find out," Lily promised her friend.

Lily stood in the center of the amusement park and made an announcement. "I don't want to frighten anyone, but it appears that there are an abundance of creepers in Lisimi Village and this amusement park, Lisimi Land. We have to be very careful."

The townspeople all talked at once. Everyone was worried if they were under attack. Michael asked, "Is it a griefer?"

"We don't know," Lily replied.

A familiar voice called out from the distance, "I think I can give you some answers."

Lily was stunned. "Georgia? How did you get back on this server?"

2
THE RETURN

"I'm not happy to be back here." Georgia burst into tears.

"How did you get back here?" Lily repeated and ran toward her old friend.

"When I was zapped back home, it was fantastic. Although I did miss all of you guys, it was so nice to sleep in my old bed and see my family. I got to play with my dog—" Georgia's sobs grew louder and nobody could understand her.

"Calm down." Lily reassured her friend. "It's going to be okay. Mr. Anarchy is working on a way to get us all off this server."

"Mr. Anarchy? But isn't he a bad guy?" Georgia was confused.

"Yes, he used to be. But he's changed, and he's very close to getting us off this server," explained Lily.

7

Georgia calmed down and explained how she became trapped on this server. "I was playing Minecraft on a new server. I was even playing in creative mode. After being trapped on this server, all I wanted to do was build and not battle." Georgia took a deep breath and continued, "But there was a rainstorm and I was shutting down my computer when I was shocked by an electric charge. When I woke up, I was back in Lisimi Village. The first place I spotted was Juan's butcher shop."

"Who zapped her on the server?" asked Lily.

"I knew it!" Simon was infuriated. "I knew there was another griefer on this server."

Mr. Anarchy said, "I don't think it was a griefer. I might be responsible for zapping Georgia onto this server."

"What?" exclaimed Lily.

"How?" questioned Michael.

"I don't understand. I thought you were good." Georgia looked at Mr. Anarchy. She wanted to know why he'd tear her away from her happy life and force her to live on this server again. It wasn't fair.

The townspeople were angry with Mr. Anarchy. One of them shouted, "I told you he'd be back to his old tricks."

Another called out, "I knew we should have never trusted him."

Lily wanted to defend Mr. Anarchy, but even she was suspicious.

The townspeople grabbed their bow and arrows and swords and pointed them at Mr. Anarchy.

He cried, "I can explain."

"You better do it fast." Peter held his bow and arrow. He unleashed one arrow that pierced Mr. Anarchy's shoulder.

"Please, stop," pleaded Mr. Anarchy.

Lily calmed everyone down. "Please let him speak. We can't prove he's guilty unless he's had a chance to explain."

The townspeople put down their weapons and waited for an explanation.

Mr. Anarchy spoke, "When I was experimenting with ways to get us off this server, I had to test some of my old methods. When I was doing that, I think I zapped Georgia back on this server, while Warren was zapped back to the real world."

"So a new person has to be zapped onto this server for another to leave?" asked Lily.

Mr. Anarchy frowned. "It looks like that might be the case with Georgia's reappearance and Warren's disappearance. I think it's a glitch. As I said, I hadn't even summoned the lightning. I was just experimenting."

"That's awful," Lily remarked.

"I feel terrible about it all," Mr. Anarchy sighed.

"Well, at least Warren is back in the real world." Georgia wiped the tears from her eyes.

Michael screamed, "Lily, watch out!"

Lily turned around as a gang of creepers silently crept up behind her. Several of them exploded next to Lily and she was destroyed.

It was still daylight when Lily respawned in her bed. She raced to the window and spotted numerous creepers lurking through the streets of Lisimi Village. While walking toward the door, she heard Robin call out, "Lily?"

"Robin, were you destroyed by the creepers, too?" Lily walked over to her friend.

Robin climbed out of the bed. "Something isn't right."

"What do you mean?"

"Warren's disappearance and the sudden creeper invasion—I'm beginning to question Mr. Anarchy's motives or if there is another griefer trying to attack us. It just doesn't make sense."

"Maybe it's a glitch? Maybe Mr. Anarchy just set something off when he was experimenting?" Lily wanted to believe Mr. Anarchy. He had proven that he was a good person.

"I don't know," said Robin. "But we have to figure out who or what is behind this. Let's find Mr. Anarchy and have him take us to his lab where he's been experimenting with the command blocks."

"That's a great idea," Lily remarked, and the two hurried toward Lisimi Land to search for Mr. Anarchy.

As Lily and Robin ran through the town, they kept a close watch for creepers. Every time they spotted a creeper, Lily would aim her bow and arrow at the hostile mob.

Robin looked up at the sky. "It's getting dark. We don't have that much time."

Lily could see Lisimi Land in the distance. "We don't have that much further to travel."

"Let's get there and try to end this creeper battle quickly. We don't want hostile mobs to spawn and also attack us, then we'll never win." Robin sprinted as fast as she could.

"Lily!" Michael called out from the entrance to Lisimi Land. "Over here!"

"We're coming," Robin said breathlessly.

"Michael, have you see Mr. Anarchy?" asked Lily.

"Yes," Michael replied. "He's battling creepers with the others. Are you going to help?"

"Yes," Lily replied and followed Michael into Lisimi Land.

"It's nonstop," Michael explained as they entered the amusement park. "We just want to destroy all of these creepers and get to safety."

Lily spotted Mr. Anarchy and she raced toward him with Robin trailing behind her. "We need to get back to your lab. We have to get to the bottom of this," she told him.

"We can't abandon everyone in the middle of the battle." Mr. Anarchy struck another creeper with his arrow and it exploded.

The constant explosions were deafening, making it hard for Lily to be heard. "I think we should leave the others to fight this battle and we should see if we can stop it. If this is somehow related to your experiment, it might be better for us to go back to the command blocks," Lily said to Mr. Anarchy as she destroyed multiple creepers.

"It's our only hope." Robin urged Mr. Anarchy to listen to Lily.

"Okay," Mr. Anarchy agreed.

Lily, Robin, and Mr. Anarchy ran from the park, but stopped in their tracks when they heard someone call out, "Guys, stop. It's me, Warren."

3
JEEPERS, CREEPERS

"**W**arren? What are you doing here?" Mr. Anarchy was stunned.

"We thought you were back in the real world?" questioned Lily.

"I was, but someone zapped me back on this server," Warren cried.

"Who?" Mr. Anarchy walked over to Warren.

"Was it Pablo, Ronan, or Matthew?" asked Robin.

"Ouch!" Mr. Anarchy grabbed his arm. "Someone hit me with an arrow."

Lily spotted a stranger. His dark brown hair covered one of his eyes, making him look like a cyclops. The one-eyed person was wearing a red sparkly jacket skin and hiding behind a tree. He rushed toward them.

"That's him! He trapped me in an abandoned mine. He's evil." Warren raced after the one-eyed person, but the one-eyed griefer splashed a potion of invisibility and disappeared.

Lily looked at Warren. "Do you know anything about this one-eyed person?"

"Yes." Warren rattled off facts about this new griefer, "His name is Nicholas, and he lives in the jungle biome. He has set up a house near an abandoned mine."

"Is he working alone?" questioned Mr. Anarchy.

"As far as I know he is," said Warren.

Lily scanned the area as she spoke; she hoped Nicholas's potion would wear off and they'd see him. She started to lose hope and asked Warren, "Do you remember where he lives? Can you lead us there?"

"Yes," Warren said. "It's not far from here."

Robin looked up at the sky. "We can't go now. It's getting too dark and it's dangerous."

"We can't wait until morning. We have to find him and stop him. We have no idea what he's plotting." Lily wanted to annihilate this evil griefer. She was also fearful because he had the power to zap people onto the server. Lily thought Mr. Anarchy was the only person smart enough to do this, and she was scared they were battling a very skilled griefer.

As evening set in, four skeletons spawned in the darkness. One of the skeletons shot an arrow at Lily.

"I told you we should get back to the cottage," Robin remarked as she leapt at the bony beasts with her diamond sword.

Lily struck one of the skeletons with her sword, destroying it. As she picked up the bone, it dropped on the ground and she heard a powerful roar.

"The Ender Dragon!" Mr. Anarchy cried out.

Robin aimed her bow and arrow at the flying beast, hitting the side of its scaly grey wing.

A new crop of skeletons spawned in the distance as zombies lumbered down a hill toward the group.

"We're going to be destroyed," Warren cried. "And I'll respawn in that prison."

Robin told Warren, "Run as fast as you can to the cottage and sleep there. We need to know that you'll respawn in Lisimi Village."

"I can't sleep if there are hostile mobs nearby," Warren reminded her.

Lily handed Warren a potion of strength. "You're right. Drink this. You need to be strong. We won't let you get destroyed."

Robin saw Michael, Simon, Ilana, Sunny, and Blossom fleeing from Lisimi Village.

"Guys, help over here!" Robin called to her friends.

The gang saw Robin battling the tricky Ender Dragon and quickly raced to her side.

Arrows shot through the sky as they tried to defeat the Ender Dragon before the skeletons and zombies unleashed a deadly attack on them.

"This is impossible," Lily screamed as she was repeatedly struck by arrows from the horde of skeletons while attempting to defeat the Ender Dragon.

Michael said, "Don't worry. We'll help you."

"How?" Lily questioned. They were outnumbered and she didn't even have time to tell Michael about the new evil griefer that was on the server.

Simon shot an arrow at the Ender Dragon when he saw Warren. "Warren. How did you get here?"

"It's a long story," Warren wearily replied as he struck the Ender Dragon with his diamond sword, but the dragon flew away.

The dragon unleashed a loud roar and flew toward Warren. He tried to grab the potion of strength, but he didn't have time. The dragon's wing struck Warren and he lost a heart. He tried to grab the potion again, but three skeletons shot arrows at him. As the arrows ripped through his arm, Warren lost his final heart and was destroyed.

"Warren!" Lily cried.

"He must be back in the jungle prison," Robin shouted. "We have to find him."

Michael pierced the dragon with his diamond sword, and the beast was destroyed. He reached over to pick up the dragon's egg and almost tripped onto the portal to the End.

"Watch out!" Robin cried.

Michael thought Robin was talking about the portal, when she was actually warning him that six creepers were right behind him.

Kaboom!

The creepers detonated and Michael was obliterated.

Simon struck the final skeleton that battled them. "Now that we've destroyed all the hostile mobs, can somebody explain how Warren got back on this server?"

"In the morning," Lily replied and she sprinted back to the safety of her cottage. The others followed.

4
NETHER ESCAPE

ily ran to the window. The sun was shining, as she called out to Robin, "We have to find the others and rescue Warren."

Robin put on armor and they raced to find their friends, but when they reached the center of town, it was empty. Lily wondered if everyone was hiding from the creeper invasion, but was relieved when she spotted Michael and Sunny in the center of town.

Lily called out to them, "Are you coming with us?"

"Yes," Michael said. "We're waiting for Simon, Peter, Ilana, and Blossom."

The others emerged from the blacksmith shop. Ilana remarked, "I think we have enough weapons. I feel prepared."

"Do you have potions?" asked Lily.

Ilana was a well-known alchemist and had a bunch of potions on hand. "Yes, do you need some?"

Lily took out the diamonds she had in her inventory and traded them for potions.

"I think we're ready to go." Michael studied his inventory as he spoke.

"What about Mr. Anarchy? We need him. He's probably the only one who could defeat this new one-eyed griefer," said Lily.

"He must be in his lab." Robin walked toward Mr. Anarchy's lab, which was housed in an old library.

There was a stronghold underneath the library where he carried out his experiments. Mr. Anarchy had tested various ways of leaving the server and felt he was finally close to getting everyone back home.

Lily walked into the lab. "Mr. Anarchy?"

Mr. Anarchy was working with a couple of command blocks. "Oh good, you're here."

"We have to stop Nicholas and save Warren," Lily told her friend.

"I'm ready." Mr. Anarchy armored up and sprinted out of the lab.

As they traveled to the jungle biome, Lily expressed her concerns about the new griefer, "He's the only other person who is able to zap people onto this server. I'm really worried. I didn't want anyone else to get trapped on here."

"Me either," Mr. Anarchy agreed. "But I think I know a way we could stop him."

"How?" questioned Simon.

"I'm going to experiment with a new technique I've been working on. I'm going to zap him off the server.

Or at the very least, I'm going to destroy his command blocks. Without those, he won't be able to zap anyone onto the server," explained Mr. Anarchy.

Large trees loomed in the distance. They approached a calm river.

"I can see the jungle," Peter called out.

"Great, we're almost there." Lily asked, "Does anyone know how we're going to find Nicholas's house?"

"I'm not sure." Peter suggested, "I can clear a path, so we can explore the biome."

The gang explored the jungle biome. Ilana called out, "I see a jungle temple."

A large jungle temple stood on the foot of the river. Michael stopped and stared at the jungle temple, "We should go in. We can find some treasure."

"Treasure will be worthless to us soon," Mr. Anarchy reminded him. "We will be back in the real world and starting again on a new server."

Lily agreed. "Right now we have to concentrate on stopping Nicholas and getting back home."

Ilana called out in a panicked voice, "I don't see Peter. Does anybody see him?"

Sunny and Blossom searched the leafy path. Sunny said, "Don't worry. I see him in the distance."

"Me too!" Blossom sprinted toward Peter.

As they approached their friend, they realized he was in the middle of a battle with the one-eyed griefer.

"Stop!" Mr. Anarchy screamed at Nicholas.

"Never," Nicholas laughed as he struck Peter with his diamond sword.

Peter was extremely weak. Lily wanted to hand him a potion of healing, but she didn't have the chance. As creepers spawned, they silently crept close to Lily and exploded. Lily's hearts were depleted. She didn't even have a chance to fight back. She was destroyed.

When Lily respawned in her house, she looked for Robin, but she wasn't there. Lily assumed Robin was still in the jungle and decided to TP back to her friends. As she began to TP, Lily heard a loud explosion.

"Lily," Robin shouted at Lily. "Watch out!"

Lily emerged in the jungle biome near a group of creepers. Luckily Lily was able to escape this creeper invasion and she raced toward Nicholas and ripped into his chest with her diamond sword.

Nicholas lost a heart. "You think you're going to win, don't you?"

"Yes," Mr. Anarchy shouted and he rushed toward Nicholas with a potion of weakness.

"Warren," Nicholas shouted. "Ignite the portal."

Lily and the others were stunned when Warren quickly crafted a portal to the Nether. They watched him run toward the portal and disappear with Nicholas.

As purple mist surrounded them, Lily called out, "Warren? What are you doing?"

He didn't respond. He was already in the fiery Nether biome.

"Do you think Warren is working with Nicholas?" questioned Ilana.

"I don't know." Lily stood speechless.

"There's only one way we're going to find out." Mr. Anarchy started to craft a portal to the Nether. "I need more obsidian."

Peter grabbed obsidian from his inventory and placed it on the ground, completing the rectangle.

The group huddled together as they ignited the portal and traveled to the Nether.

When they emerged in the red Nether landscape, the gang spawned by a large lava waterfall. Lily looked out for ghasts and blazes.

Peter walked a bit further from the group, exploring the biome, and called out, "I see a Nether fortress."

"We have to find Nicholas and Warren," Lily reminded him.

"I know," Peter said. "But we have no idea where they might be."

"Maybe we shouldn't have traveled to the Nether." Ilana appeared defeated, but the battle hadn't even begun.

Michael looked at the fortress. "I think we should check it out. They could be in there."

Simon said, "And we could find treasure!"

The minute Simon uttered the word *treasure*, everyone started to fantasize about the various treasures that might be deep in the Nether fortress.

Lily didn't want to search for treasure in the fortress, but she had to follow the others. She was outnumbered and reluctantly traveled toward the grand structure with Peter.

Three blazes guarded the fortress. Lily shot an arrow at a blaze, destroying the yellow beast. She was reaching for the blaze rod as it dropped when she heard a voice cry out for help.

Lily looked over at Mr. Anarchy. "I hear someone crying for help."

The gang battled the remaining blazes, as Lily and Mr. Anarchy snuck into the Nether fortress.

"I don't see anyone." Mr. Anarchy stood in the main room.

Lily walked down the hall. She was shocked to see Nicholas and Warren immersed in a battle dangerously close to a pool of lava.

"Quick!" she called to Mr. Anarchy. "They're in the lava room."

Warren cried for help.

"See!" Lily called out. "I knew Warren wasn't evil."

Mr. Anarchy rushed toward Warren. He looked at Lily and whispered, "I hope Warren isn't tricking us."

5

THE INVASION OF THE WITHER SKELETONS

"Warren," Lily called to her friend.

"Help me!" Warren cried.

Lily ran over to Nicholas, pounding her diamond sword into Nicholas's chest. "Stop it!" Lily pleaded.

The others entered the fortress and hurried toward Lily and helped her battle Nicholas.

Nicholas splashed a potion of harming on Peter, leaving him with one heart.

"Drink this." Ilana rushed to Peter's side with a potion.

Peter gulped the potion and used his renewed energy to strike Nicholas, leaving him with only one heart. "Gotcha!"

Mr. Anarchy delivered the final blow and Nicholas was destroyed.

"We have to stop him," Warren said breathlessly as he grabbed a potion of healing from his inventory.

"Can you lead us to the jungle?" Mr. Anarchy questioned Warren.

"Yes, I know where *he* is," Warren started to say, but before he could finish his sentence, a swarm of wither skeletons spawned in the dimly lit fortress.

Lily sprinted away in an attempt to dodge one of the spawning wither skeleton's powerful stone sword, but the dark skeleton struck her and she was hit with the Wither effect. Lily was weak and could barely gather enough strength to hold her diamond sword or pick milk from her inventory to restore her energy. She watched as the others tried to battle the wither skeletons, but one by one, each of her friends was struck with the Wither effect.

Warren was able to sip milk and restore his health. He struck a wither skeleton and defeated the dark, bony Nether mob. "It dropped a stone sword!" Warren exclaimed, noting the rare find.

Three wither skeletons surrounded Lily. She tried to battle them, but she was outnumbered. Lily clutched her diamond sword, but she dropped it while leaping at the wither skeleton. Two skeletons lunged at Lily and plowed their stone swords into her arm. Lily was destroyed. As she faded, Lily saw one of the wither skeletons pick up her diamond sword.

Lily respawned in bed. She wanted to get back to the Nether fortress to help her friends battle the evil skeletons, but there was somebody standing beside her bed.

"Lily," the sinister voice said with a snicker, "it's just you and me. What an easy battle."

Lily panicked. She didn't have her diamond sword, although her inventory was full of potions she had gotten from Ilana.

Lily cried out, "Nicholas, what do you want from me? What do you want from any of us? Can't you see that being a griefer is just plain mean? Even Mr. Anarchy changed his ways and learned that it's better to work with people than against them."

"I don't need to hear one of your speeches about good and evil. I know what I want. I want to take over this server."

"But don't you want to go home? Don't you want to leave this server?" Lily questioned, hoping this would humanize Nicholas.

"No, I never want to go home. When I go back home, I'm just a kid who has to go to school every day and do chores. Here, I am master of the world. I can stay here forever and be king."

"But it's not real," Lily uttered, but these words infuriated Nicholas.

He struck Lily with his diamond sword, until she only had one heart left. "You're defenseless," he laughed.

Lily stared at Nicholas; she tried not to look over at Robin, who had respawned in her bed, and quietly walked over to Nicholas. When Robin was close enough, she splashed a potion of harming on him and then struck him with his diamond sword. Lily grabbed a potion from her inventory and threw it on Nicholas. He was destroyed.

Lily looked at Robin. "I don't have a diamond sword. One of the wither skeletons has it."

Robin looked through her inventory. "I have an extra one. Take it."

"I can't do that," Lily said. "That's too valuable."

"No gift is too valuable for a friend." Robin handed Lily the sword.

"Thanks," Lily said, "but can I trade you for it? I just feel awkward taking it."

"Okay, you can trade two emeralds for it."

"That's not enough," Lily said as she retrieved two emeralds from her inventory and handed them to Robin.

"That's all I'm willing to take. And anyway, this stuff will be meaningless soon. Once Mr. Anarchy figures out a way to get us off this server, we'll be able to go on new missions to refill our inventories. We'll be on a new server and we'll just play a game, not live it."

Lily hoped Robin was right. She was beginning to lose hope, but she didn't want anybody to know this fact. She smiled. "You're right. We'll be home soon."

As these words fell from Lily's lips, Nicholas burst through the door. "I'm back and you're my prisoners!" he screamed at Lily and Robin.

6

HOME SWEET HOME

Lily gasped as she watched Nicholas construct a bedrock wall inside her house. "There's no way to escape now. You'll be trapped in here forever! I hope you have a lot of food."

Robin screamed, "Stop!" She pleaded with Nicholas, "Don't finish this wall. You're being a bully."

"I know," Nicholas laughed as he finished the wall, boxing the two into a small space.

"What are we going to do?" Lily paced in the small bedrock prison.

"I don't know," Robin said. "But I know the others will come looking for us. Maybe they'll see the bedrock wall and destroy it."

"How?" Lily was annoyed. "Bedrock is impossible to destroy."

Robin paused and said, "The cube of destruction. They can use that and break down this wall and release us from prison."

"That's incredibly powerful. If they detonate the cube of destruction, my house will be destroyed. And so will we."

Robin reminded her, "We will respawn and we can rebuild the house. We just have to get out of here."

"I wonder how long we'll be stuck here." Lily grabbed a couple of apples from her inventory and handed one to Robin.

"Thanks." Robin took a bite out of the apple. "I'm sure they'll come looking for us soon."

A thunderous boom was heard outside. "I bet he summoned a storm! And we can't even help our friends." Lily was upset.

"Now they'll be so busy battling hostile mobs that they'll never be able to save us." Robin's eyes filled with tears.

Lily looked at the ground. "Nicholas isn't as smart as we think he is." She grabbed a pickaxe from her inventory and banged it against the ground.

"Oh my!" Robin looked down. "You made a hole."

"We are going to dig our way out of this." Lily smiled.

Robin grabbed her pickaxe and broke away at the blocky ground. She looked down at the hole. "We're making lots of progress."

"Soon, we'll be able to crawl in and dig our way into Lisimi Village." Lily used all of her strength to make the hole large enough to fit through. Once the hole was the right size, she hopped in and Robin joined her.

"I have a torch." Robin placed her torch in the tunnel.

"That helps," Lily said enthusiastically. "We don't have to go too far."

"Yes." Robin hit the ceiling and saw a glimmer of light. "It looks like the rain has stopped."

The two worked furiously to break through the roof and climb into Lisimi Village. Robin was the first to climb to safety. Lily followed; she looked out and saw the shore.

"We're on the beach," Lily remarked.

Emily the Fisherwoman was on the shore, fishing. "Lily and Robin, you have to get to safety. There's a new griefer terrorizing Lisimi Village. I'm placing all of my fish in my inventory and trying to find a safe place to hide."

Lily looked through her inventory. After dropping and giving up her diamond sword, she began to worry that she might lose other items from her inventory. She looked over at Robin. "Do you think we should store some of our resources in an Ender chest?"

"That sounds like a good plan, but where will we put it?" questioned Robin.

Emily the Fisherwoman suggested, "There's a stronghold near a mine right outside of town. You should put it there." Emily showed them a map and pointed out the stronghold.

Lily and Robin studied the map and started toward the stronghold.

"It looks like it's right here." Robin pointed to a cave.

"Let's go in." Lily walked into the abandoned mine and searched for the stronghold.

"Over here!" Robin called out.

"Watch out!" warned Lily.

Two skeletons spawned in the stronghold. Lily shot an arrow at one of the bony beasts, but lost a heart when a cluster of silverfish crawled by her feet and attacked her. "Robin, there are too many silverfish over here. You have to battle the skeletons on your own."

"I'll try," Robin gasped. The skeletons were vicious and shot a barrage of arrows that struck Robin's body.

Lily put her bow and arrow back in her inventory and took out the diamond sword. She furiously struck the small silverfish that carpeted the dirty floor. Lily knew there had to be a silverfish spawner close by, but she didn't want to search for it while Robin battled the skeletons on her own.

"Help!" Robin called out. She was down to two hearts and the skeletons weren't backing off.

Lily pulled a potion from her inventory and splashed it on the skeletons, as she ordered Robin, "Strike them now!"

Robin fumbled with her diamond sword.

Lily cried, "Don't drop it!"

Robin regained her footing and struck one of the skeletons until it was destroyed.

Lily stood by Robin's side and destroyed the second skeleton. "I hope we don't have to deal with any more skeletons."

Robin took milk from her inventory and handed it to Lily. "We have to drink this—both of us are very weak."

Lily took a sip. "We must look for the silverfish spawner."

Robin paused. "Do you think we made a mistake coming to this stronghold? Should we have stayed in Lisimi Village and helped our friends?"

"I think we've exhausted our inventories many times and this was a good idea. Now we'll have an Ender chest filled with resources that are invaluable in helping us battle this new griefer."

"I guess you're right," Robin said as the two searched for the silverfish spawner. The hall was dark and they kept an eye out for more hostile mobs that might spawn in the stronghold.

"We have to craft that Ender chest," Lily remarked as they explored the musty stronghold.

"Why don't we do it now? I have obsidian and the Eyes of Ender," Robin suggested. "We can just make it and fill it with twenty-seven pieces from our inventory."

"Good idea," Lily agreed, but when a horde of silverfish crawled toward them, she knew they had to continue their search for the spawner.

"I think I see the spawner," Robin crept toward a dark corner of the stronghold. "Follow me."

"I see it, too!" Lily called out.

The two broke the spawner and let out a collective sigh of relief. "Now we can build that Ender chest." Robin smiled.

They gathered the supplies from their inventories and crafted the chest. As they each placed vital items from their inventories into the Ender chest, they heard voices in the stronghold.

"Do you hear that?" questioned Lily.

"Yes." Robin picked up her pace and filled the Ender chest. "We have to hide the Ender chest."

Lily placed it into the dark corner. "It should be fine here."

The voices grew louder. There was a sliver of light emanating from the ceiling and Lily walked over to the small patch of light, hoping she'd be able to see who was in the stronghold.

Lily gasped.

"Do you see them?' questioned Robin.

Lily whispered, "Yes, I'm really scared."

7
EXPLOSIVE ENEMIES

"**W**ho is it?" Robin was too afraid to look.
Kaboom!
A slew of creepers detonated, destroying them, and the two friends were back in the cottage and behind the bedrock wall.

Lily looked down at the ground and was relieved to see the hole was still there.

Robin leapt out of bed and jumped into the hole; Lily followed.

"Who did you see in the stronghold?" Robin asked as she placed a torch on the dirt wall.

"I know it sounds crazy, but I think I saw Pablo, Ronan, and Matthew." Lily couldn't believe she was uttering these words.

"Really? They've escaped from prison?" Robin questioned while sprinting through the tunnel.

"I don't know," Lily wondered. "Maybe they're working with Nicholas?"

"Oh no!" Robin shuddered. "I guess we have an even bigger battle to fight."

"This is awful," Lily remarked as they crawled out of the tunnel and onto the shore.

"We should see if we can find any of our friends," Robin said.

Lily was already looking off in the distance, hoping she'd see Simon or Michael, but the town looked empty. "I don't see anyone."

Robin suggested, "Let's go to Juan's butcher shop and see if he has seen anyone in the town."

"Good idea!" Lily exclaimed and they set off for the village.

"Robin! Lily!" a voice called out.

"Michael!" Lily was thrilled to see her friends. "And Simon!"

Michael spoke quickly, "Everyone is trapped in the jungle. Nicholas has awful plans for them. Mr. Anarchy tried to reason with him, but it didn't work."

Simon added, "Nicholas is pure evil."

Lily said, "We have to go to the jungle and help everyone."

"Yes," Michael said. "We were just on our way there."

Lily suggested they TP to the jungle and everyone agreed that was the best plan. As they emerged in the thick of a jungle path, dense with leaves, Lily dodged a fireball. "What was that?" she cried out.

"It looked like a fireball from a ghast." Robin searched the sky, but it was hard to see because of the leaves.

"Oh no! I hope Nicholas didn't spawn Nether mobs in the Overworld." Lily's voice shook as she spoke.

"He has," Michael replied.

"And we had to battle the Wither," Simon told Lily and Robin.

"Twice," Michael reminded him.

"He's not joking around. He does want to terrorize us," Lily remarked.

"We can't let him distract us with these hostile mobs; we have to pay attention and focus on freeing our friends," Michael said.

Another fireball shot through the leaves. Lily struck the fireball with her fist and hoped it would strike the fiery beast. She wanted to tell Michael and Simon that she thought she saw Pablo, Ronan, and Matthew in the stronghold, but she knew this wasn't the time. They had to concentrate and battle these hostile mobs so they could free their friends.

"There are ghasts!" Robin screeched.

"Tons of them," Lily cried as she saw several ghasts through the leaves.

"I wish we had snowballs," Simon said as he aimed his bow and arrow.

Michael was annoyed. "We used up all of our snowballs fighting the Wither."

Lily looked through her inventory. She didn't have any snowballs. Robin also checked and didn't have any, either.

"We don't have snowballs," Lily remarked. "We're just going to have to use our fists and our bow and arrows."

The gang battled the ghasts, but it wasn't easy. The flying fiery mobs shot countless fireballs at the group, and the gang was growing weaker by the minute.

"We have to save our friends. This is getting very annoying," Lily yelped as she struck another fireball with her fist and destroyed yet another ghast.

"Nicholas isn't playing around," Michael said as he dodged a blast. "I have no idea what he's planning for our friends, but I'm sure it's going to be terrible."

Simon looked up at the sky and there was hope in his voice when he said, "It looks like there are only a couple of more ghasts left to destroy."

Lily used her last bit of strength to defeat the ghasts that flew above them. "Now lead us to our friends," she ordered Michael.

Michael and Simon sheared a path toward the prison where their friends were being kept prisoner.

"It's over here," Michael said quietly.

They walked to a tree with a large hole in its bark, and Michael was about to climb in when Lily suggested, "Should we splash a potion of invisibility on ourselves? We don't want Nicholas seeing us."

"Good idea." Michael grabbed the potion from his inventory.

"I hope it isn't booby-trapped," Simon said.

"Me too!" Robin agreed.

Before they splashed the potion, Lily spotted Pablo, Ronan, and Matthew rushing toward them.

"Oh no!" Lily gasped. "Here comes trouble."

8
CONFRONTATIONS

Simon pointed his diamond sword at Pablo, Ronan, and Matthew and hollered, "What do you want?"

"We've come to help," Pablo confessed.

Lily was suspicious. "Help us? Really?"

Ronan explained, "Nicholas released us from prison. He wanted us to help him take over this server. We agreed to help him, but as we worked with him, we realized that he was one of the scariest people we've ever met."

"How?" questioned Lily. She didn't believe Ronan.

"He wanted us to put Ilana on command blocks and then destroy her while the others watched. He wanted to show them that he could erase them from existence," added Matthew.

"You've tried to do that to us. Why do you think that's such a big deal?" asked Michael.

"The real reason is Nicholas doesn't want to go home," Pablo said.

Ronan interrupted him, "He wants to zap everyone he can onto the server and just torment them. He is trying to build a large prison in which to put anyone who doesn't agree with his plans."

"How will he do this alone?" questioned Simon.

"He is zapping people on now. He is creating an enormous army," said Ronan.

"He zapped more people onto the server?" Lily was infuriated.

"Yes, he zapped two people when we were working with him." Ronan choked back the tears. "I just want to go home. I'm sorry I was a griefer. I just want to get off this server."

"If only we could rescue Mr. Anarchy. He was on the verge of figuring out how we can get off of this server." Lily wanted to free Mr. Anarchy. She knew he'd be able to help them.

"Nicholas will never free Mr. Anarchy." Ronan sniffled. "He is the most powerful person on this server. Nicholas is going to force him to work with him."

"But how? Mr. Anarchy isn't a griefer anymore." Lily was confused.

"Nicholas is very tricky; he will use some tactic to make Mr. Anarchy a griefer again," Matthew said.

Lily was starting to trust Pablo, Ronan, and Matthew. She asked, "How can you help us?"

Simon added, "How can you prove that you're not griefers anymore?"

Michael said, "It took a long time for Mr. Anarchy to prove his dedication and to convince us that he's good."

Pablo stuttered, "Can't you just believe us? Can't you take our word?"

"Your word!" Michael laughed.

There was no time to discuss the griefers' motives and whether this trio was trustworthy or not because a large blue monster flew through the sky, distracting the gang.

"It's the Wither!" Michael yelled.

"Not again," Simon sighed.

"We don't have any snowballs." Robin was upset. She aimed her bow and arrow at the three-headed beast, but she knew it was pointless. The Wither was impossible to battle.

Lily was shocked when Pablo handed her a stack of snowballs. "Use these; I have a bunch."

Lily handed a few snowballs to Robin and they threw them at the beast. A fiery wither skull shot through the leaves and the blast struck Lily, leaving her with the dreadful Wither effect. Lily stood motionless and exhausted, and her hearts turned black and were depleted.

Ronan sprinted to Lily and offered her milk. Lily gulped the milk and replenished her inventory. She was beginning to trust these griefers.

Michael and Simon struck the beast with snowballs and weakened the powerful flying mob, but it was still strong enough to shoot countless wither skulls at the gang. Robin was also struck by a wither skull and experienced the Wither effect. Matthew gave her milk, as he used his other hand to slam a snowball into the Wither.

"We're weakening it," Simon called out hopefully.

Lily used her last snowball to strike the Wither. The snowball destroyed the Wither, as the beast dropped a Nether star.

Lily sprinted toward the falling Nether star and placed it in her inventory. "Is it okay that I took the Nether star?" she asked the others.

"Yes." Pablo smiled.

Michael declared, "Let's go free the others from Nicholas's prison."

Everyone splashed a potion of invisibility on themselves, and one by one they crawled into the hole on the side of the tree. Lily was slightly worried that Pablo, Ronan, and Matthew might be deceiving them, but they had proved themselves in the battle against the Wither, and she had to trust them. They needed as much help as they could to battle Nicholas. Lily was also happy that they didn't have to worry about these griefers.

As they walked deeper into the cave and made their way to the stronghold, Lily worried the potion would wear off before they were able to find their friends.

"I don't see anything," Michael whispered. "I thought the prison was right down this hallway."

"Look out," Lily cried out in a hushed voice. "There are cave spiders lurking around this place."

A pair of red eyes stared at Lily. She struck the cave spider with her diamond sword and kept a close eye for other pesky bugs that were in the stronghold.

"Over here!" Simon exclaimed.

"Quiet!" Michael warned him. "Keep your voice down."

"But I found the entrance." Simon couldn't hide his excitement.

"I know, but we don't want Nicholas to hear us," Michael reminded him.

A voice screamed through the darkness, "Too late!"

Lily turned around and saw Nicholas's red jacket sparkle in the darkness. She lunged toward Nicholas, ripping through his sparkly red jacket, and since she was still invisible, he was completely vulnerable to the surprise attack.

9
FREEDOM

"**L**et our friends go!" Lily shouted as she continued to strike Nicholas's one-eyed skin with her diamond sword.

Nicholas couldn't see Lily and tried to strike her with his diamond sword, but her invisibility gave her an advantage and she was easily able to dodge the strikes from his sword.

"It's wearing off," Michael warned Lily as he saw her reappear.

"Now I've got you." Nicholas leapt at Lily and cornered her against a wall in the stronghold.

Lily didn't warn Nicholas that three creepers were silently lurking behind him. The silent creepers exploded, weakening Nicholas. Robin slammed her sword into Nicholas and he was destroyed.

Michael rushed to the door and freed his friends.

Ilana was the first to sprint out. "Thank you!"

Peter, Sunny, Blossom, and Warren hurried out of the prison.

"Warren?" Lily questioned. "I thought you were working with Nicholas?"

"No, he isn't," Peter replied. "I'll explain."

Lily couldn't listen to Peter's explanation. She wanted to know where Mr. Anarchy was hiding. She walked into the small prison and didn't see him in the room.

"Where's Mr. Anarchy?" Lily was stunned to see the room was empty.

Peter called out, "He's in his own prison. We don't know where, but Nicholas took him out and had him work on a project."

Warren warned them, "He zapped other people onto the server. He made them change their skins and they are all one-eyed and wear sparkly jackets like him. Nicholas said something about how he had met other one-eyed griefers when he was playing the game once, and he wanted to replicate their power on this server."

"That's awful!" Lily cried out, but then questioned Warren. "Why did you help Nicholas craft a portal to the Nether?"

"I was afraid of him," Warren confessed. "I didn't want him to hurt you and I know he can be very evil."

Three griefers sporting sparkly jackets emerged from down the hall and shot arrows at the group. Ilana splashed a potion of weakness on them, and Lily leapt at the griefers with her diamond sword.

Warren had other plans. He tried to talk to the weakened griefers. "You don't have to be evil. I know Nicholas zapped you onto this server. He did the same thing to me. You don't have to follow his rules."

Ilana added, "Nicholas never wants to leave this server. We want to leave. If you stick with us, you will hopefully make your way back to the real world."

Peter said, "If you stick with Nicholas you'll be here forever. He'll never let you leave."

One griefer, who wore a purple sparkly jacket, put his sword down. "You mean he wants us to stay here forever and never go back home?"

The other two griefers, one dressed in a blue jacket and another in an orange one, were annoyed at their friend for questioning Nicholas. The blue griefer struck the purple-jacketed griefer with his diamond sword.

"Stop!" Lily screamed at the blue and orange griefers. "How can you follow Nicholas? He's not going to help you escape. I have no idea what he promised you, but it's not worth it."

"He told us that we will be able to control this server forever, that we will be the kings," admitted the blue griefer.

"But we'll never get to leave the server," the purple griefer said to his friend.

"Who cares?" the blue griefer replied.

"You're right—we will be powerful forever." The purple griefer grinned.

Peter called out, "But that's awful. Don't you want to leave? Don't you miss your home?"

The blue griefer smiled and struck Peter with his sword. "Yeah, but this is a lot more fun."

"Attacking you guys is super awesome," the blue griefer cackled as he struck Ilana, Robin, and Michael with his sword.

"You'll grow bored of it, I promise," Simon told them as he struck the two griefers.

"Doubt it," the blue griefer replied and engaged in a skilled sword battle with Simon.

Lily was battling the griefers when she stopped. She could hear Mr. Anarchy's cries in the distance. "I have to save my friend."

"Your friend," said the orange griefer, "is about to be wiped from existence."

"No!" Lily cried and tried to run toward Mr. Anarchy, but the orange griefer lunged at her with his diamond sword, while the blue griefer splashed a potion of weakness on her. Lily was losing hearts. She tried to fight back, but she didn't see the two skeletons that spawned behind her. They unleashed a sea of arrows that struck Lily's back and she was destroyed.

Lily's heart was racing as she respawned in her bed. She looked over at Robin, who had just respawned in her bed.

"Who destroyed the bedrock wall? Look." Lily pointed out the rubble. "They must have used the cube of destruction, and it didn't even cause that much damage to our house," Lily noticed a few small blocky holes, which were easily repairable.

"I bet Michael or Simon or someone else thought we were trapped in here and were trying to free us," suggested Robin.

Lily agreed.

Lily looked out the window and realized it was nighttime. They must have lost track of time in the stronghold and didn't realize it was the middle of the night.

A zombie ripped Lily's door from the hinges. She wanted to TP back to the stronghold, but didn't have a chance. Three zombies entered her living room and she had to destroy them.

Lily grabbed her diamond sword and struck one of the vacant-eyed mobs. The three zombies surrounded her. Lily quickly took out a potion of harming and splashed the zombies, but it didn't destroy them. The zombies grabbed her and she lost a heart. Lily was worried; she'd be destroyed and by the time she could respawn back to the stronghold, Mr. Anarchy would be destroyed. She hoped her friends were able to battle the griefers and save Mr. Anarchy.

Lily splashed another potion on the zombies, and one of the undead beasts was destroyed, but she saw others lumbering toward her cottage. Lily was trapped.

"Lily," Robin called out.

"Help!" Lily cried.

Robin slammed her sword into the swarm of zombies, annihilating the undead mob with her strength.

Lily had a moment to grab a potion from her inventory and sip it to regain her energy. "Let's destroy these zombies," Lily shouted as more zombies entered the small cottage.

Robin and Lily struck the zombies with their swords and used potions to weaken the undead mob. When the final zombie was destroyed, Robin said, "I have to tell you something. It's about Mr. Anarchy."

10

TESTING

"What's happened to Mr. Anarchy?" Lily asked Robin.

"I think Nicholas is performing some horrendous experiment on him," Robin informed her friend.

The two TPed back to the jungle and Robin called to Michael, "Over here!"

Michael rushed toward them, but the blue-and orange-jacketed griefers raced behind Michael. The green griefer caught up to Michael and splashed a potion of weakness on him. Simon attacked the blue griefer before he had a chance to hurt Michael.

Ilana, Peter, Pablo, Ronan, Matthew, Sunny, and Blossom clutched potions and splashed them on the two griefers, destroying Nicholas's evil minions.

"We need to find Mr. Anarchy!" Lily ordered the others. "We must search every inch of this stronghold until we find him."

A pair of red eyes peered out from a corner. Lily jumped back, but it was too late and the spider bit her. The spider's poison entered Lily's body and she lost a heart. Another spider crawled toward her and bit her foot. Lily's health bar was slowly being depleted.

"Help!" Lily cried.

Michael struck the spiders with his diamond sword, obliterating the arachnids.

Simon called out, "I see a door. Maybe this is where Nicholas is keeping Mr. Anarchy?"

"Maybe!" Nicholas's voice was loud and almost deafening.

Lily leapt at Nicholas, but he laughed and splashed a potion of harming on her.

"Mr. Anarchy isn't trapped in the prison." Nicholas opened the door. "He is free to leave, but he doesn't want to go. He wants to stay here and help me terrorize you guys. Maybe you thought he's changed his ways, but he hasn't. He's still a terror."

Mr. Anarchy sat in a room tinkering with command blocks. Lily was the first to enter the room.

"Tell me Nicholas is lying. You can't be evil. You're my friend." Tears streamed down Lily's face.

Mr. Anarchy didn't look up at Lily as he worked with the command blocks.

Simon quickly entered the room. "You're evil? Why?"

Again, Mr. Anarchy didn't respond and just fixated his attention on the command blocks.

"What are you doing?" Lily pleaded. "Speak to me!"

Mr. Anarchy didn't speak; he focused on his experiment and didn't look up at anyone.

"I'm standing right here! You can't ignore me!" Lily exclaimed. She grabbed her diamond sword and pointed it at Mr. Anarchy.

Nicholas noticed and rushed toward Lily. "Leave him alone! He works for me now."

"I don't believe you." Lily struck Nicholas with her diamond sword. He lost a heart and was infuriated. Nicholas called for the three one-eyed griefers to assist him, but only the blue and orange griefer appeared. Nicholas questioned, "Where's the purple griefer?"

"He's missing," the blue griefer replied as he struck Lily with his diamond sword.

Michael and Simon raced into the small prison cell to help Lily battle Nicholas and the griefers.

Lily couldn't even concentrate on the battle; she was too bothered by Mr. Anarchy. She had trusted him and he was betraying her. She didn't know what experiment he was working on, but she knew it would hurt her friends. Lily was devastated that Nicholas was able to brainwash Mr. Anarchy.

Michael and Simon battled the two griefers, while the others crowded into the tiny cell to help defeat the griefers. Mr. Anarchy didn't pay attention to the battle that was taking places inches from him. He was immersed in finishing his experiment.

A loud thunderous boom shook the small stronghold room. The blocky ground rattled.

"It's going to explode," Nicholas cried out and ran toward the exit.

Everyone followed Nicholas, except Mr. Anarchy, who stood by the command blocks.

Nicholas looked out at the rainy sky. "I don't want to go out there. It's dangerous."

Pablo, Ronan, and Matthew held their swords against Nicholas's back. Pablo said, "You have no choice."

Pablo, Ronan and Matthew forced Nicholas out of the stronghold. As they exited the stronghold, rain fell on them. It was still nighttime, and lightning shot through the dark, cloudy sky. Nicholas, Pablo, Ronan, and Matthew were struck by the lightning.

"Where did they go?" Lily questioned.

Nicholas, Pablo, Ronan, and Matthew disappeared.

Mr. Anarchy rushed from the stronghold. "Did it work?" He looked over at Lily.

"What are you talking about?" Lily asked as she shielded herself from the rain.

"He's gone!" Mr. Anarchy smiled. "I got rid of Nicholas!"

"And Pablo, Ronan, and Matthew," added Ilana.

Mr. Anarchy raced back inside, and seconds later the storm stopped.

"Mr. Anarchy?" Lily sprinted down the dirt hall and toward Mr. Anarchy's prison cell.

He walked out of the room. "Lily, I'm sorry I was silent before, but I had just reached a vital point in my experiment and I knew that I finally found the way to get us off this server. If Nicholas thought I was working with him, I'd be able to finish it and then zap him off first."

"He's back in the real world?" asked Lily.

"So are Pablo, Ronan, and Matthew?" Simon wanted confirmation.

"Yes, I was able to zap them back," Mr. Anarchy announced proudly.

The others crowded behind Lily. The blue griefer was furious. "You destroyed Nicholas. I will never forgive you."

The orange griefer stood next to the blue griefer and declared, "I will imprison all of you. Mr. Anarchy, you're a traitor!"

"You guys are next!" Mr. Anarchy screamed and ordered the others to chase the blue griefer out of the stronghold and toward the lightning bolt. Mr. Anarchy summoned a powerful bolt with command blocks.

Lily held her sword against the blue griefer. Michael cornered the orange griefer. Both wore terrified expressions as they ran from the stronghold and were struck by lightning. Lily and Michael watched from the stronghold.

The two griefers were zapped by the lightning and returned to the real world.

Ilana rushed back into the small prison cell and confronted Mr. Anarchy. "Mr. Anarchy. Stop! It's not fair. I want to go home. Why are you rewarding the bad when the good people want to leave?"

"I needed to zap off the bad people so I can focus on getting everyone off. We don't want any distractions," Mr. Anarchy explained.

"Well, I want to go first!" Ilana whined.

"No, I do!" Peter pushed in front of Ilana.

"Who said you guys are the first to go?" Blossom was annoyed. "Sunny and I deserve to go first."

"Blossom is right. We should go first!" Sunny called out.

"Why? That doesn't make sense at all. You were one of the last people zapped onto this server," Simon said. "We've been here much longer."

The friends were in the middle of a heated argument. Everyone wanted to get zapped off first.

"Stop!" Mr. Anarchy screamed.

Nobody listened. They kept arguing. Lily looked at her friends; they were battling each other in the narrow hall in the stronghold. Lily couldn't believe these good friends were quickly turning into enemies. The gang was so busy battling, they didn't realize they exited the stronghold and were bickering in the night, leaving them exposed and vulnerable to an attack from a hostile mob. Lily took a deep breath and hoped for the best.

11

THE FIRST ONE

Warren shouted, "Everyone! Please be quiet." His voice was loud and everyone stopped talking and listened. Before Warren was able to have a rational conversation with his friends, three skeletons spawned in the thick of the night.

"Watch out!" Lily shouted. "Skeletons."

"We have to be careful; it's nighttime," Michael reminded them as he raced to the skeletons and clobbered one of the bony beasts with his diamond sword. Ilana and Peter destroyed the other skeletons.

"Let's get back in the stronghold," Warren called out to his friends. "We need shelter."

One by one, the gang entered the stronghold. Mr. Anarchy explained, "I have enough command blocks to summon three lightning bolts. Then I will have to start over."

Ilana paced down the hall of the stronghold. "So we have to choose which of us is going to go first?"

Everyone spoke at once and Lily screamed, "We can't keep battling over this. It's not getting us anywhere. We have to figure out a plan for who gets zapped back first."

"Should we put our names in a hat and see who is chosen first?" asked Peter.

"Maybe we can flip a coin?" suggested Michael.

The gang had many theories, but everything came to a halt when a loud explosion rocked the stronghold.

Kaboom!

The stronghold exploded and Lily respawned in her bed in the cottage. Lily noticed something strange—the bedrock wall was gone. It was morning and Lily looked out toward the window, when Robin called her name.

"Lily? Who blew up the stronghold?" Robin was confused.

"I have no idea who did it. Maybe Nicholas left TNT down there." Lily had a bunch of theories, but no concrete answers.

"We have to find the others and get off this server." Robin put on armor and went toward the door.

Michael and Simon were standing in front of the cottage. "Mr. Anarchy is missing."

"Do you think he was zapped off?" Lily questioned.

Simon replied, "I'm not sure. We searched all of Lisimi Village.

"And everyone was accounted for but Mr. Anarchy," added Michael.

Lily paced around the entrance of the small cottage. "This is awful. We must find him."

Lily and the gang sprinted into Lisimi Village and continued their search for Mr. Anarchy. Juan the Butcher was exiting his shop. "What are you looking for?"

Michael replied, "Juan, have you seen Mr. Anarchy?"

"Oh," Juan sighed. "Is he up to his old tricks?"

"No." Lily defended her friend. "He's missing. He's still a good guy."

"I haven't seen him, but I did see the strangest person earlier today. He came into my shop and traded emeralds for some meat."

"Why was he so strange?" questioned Robin.

"For one thing, he had one eye and he wore a sparkly purple jacket, but he acted quite bizarre." Juan described the purple griefer.

"The purple griefer!" Lily exclaimed. "Maybe he can help us find Mr. Anarchy."

"Where did he go?" Michael questioned.

"I don't know," Juan confessed.

Emily the Fisherwoman and Fred the Farmer walked toward the gang. Emily said, "You won't believe what just happened. We just met the oddest person. He asked us all sorts of strange questions."

Lily looked at Emily. "Did he have one eye and was he wearing a purple jacket?"

"What type of questions did he ask?" Michael asked them.

Emily paused. "He asked one strange question about the average time people stay on this server."

Fred said, "I told him we're on it forever."

Emily smiled. "Then he asked us one about houses."

Fred clarified, "Yes, he wanted to know if you can just stay in a house that was already built or if you have to build your own."

"Did you he where he was headed?" asked Robin.

"No," Emily replied and then questioned, "Do you know this man in the purple jacket?"

"We know who he is, and he might be able to help us track down Mr. Anarchy." Lily replied.

"We know where Mr. Anarchy is. We saw Mr. Anarchy by the shore. It looked like he was about to head under the sea," Fred the Farmer told the group.

Lily thanked them and excused her friends. "We have to go to the water to see if Mr. Anarchy is there."

As the gang headed toward the quiet shoreline, they spotted a purple sparkly jacket in the distance. Robin called out to him, but realized she didn't know his name. "Stop! The man in the purple jacket, please stop!"

The one-eyed man in the purple jacket turned around. "Wow, I was looking for you guys. What happened to Nicholas and the other people he zapped onto the server?"

Simon asked, "What's your name?"

The purple man replied, "Benji."

"Benji, they were zapped back to the real world," Robin told him.

"Really? I wish I was zapped back to the real world." Benji frowned.

"You would have been zapped back, but you were missing," explained Michael.

"I wasn't missing. I knew Nicholas was going to blow up the stronghold and I was trying to get rid of the TNT, but it didn't work. It was too late and I watched it explode. I realized most of you would respawn here, so I came to this village to look for you."

"Have you seen Mr. Anarchy?" asked Lily.

Benji didn't have to reply. Everyone turned around when they heard Mr. Anarchy call out, "Guys. Over here!"

The gang sprinted toward Mr. Anarchy. "We're so glad we found you," Lily exclaimed.

Michael questioned, "When can you zap us back to the real world?"

"I would do it right now, but all of my command blocks were destroyed in the explosion."

Benji announced, "I know where we can get command blocks. Nicholas had a bunch stored in a mineshaft in the jungle.

"Great." Mr. Anarchy asked, "Can you lead us there?"

The gang sprinted toward the jungle biome. Ilana and Warren spotted the gang in the middle of the town, and called out, "Can we join you?"

"Yes," Lily said breathlessly. "We're going to get command blocks, so we can finally get back home."

"And I don't want to hear you fight about who is going first," Mr. Anarchy said as he raced toward the leafy biome.

Large trees stood out in the verdant landscape with the lazy river running through the lush biome. Simon pointed at the oak trees. "We're almost there." The group raced into a valley filled with ripe melons.

Benji looked confused. "Maybe we made a wrong turn. I remember the mineshaft was right by this patch of melons and was covered with vines."

A familiar voice called out, "Looking for command blocks?"

"Nicholas." Mr. Anarchy was stunned. "It can't be."

12

CREEP

"I'm back on the server and ready to destroy you!" Nicholas pounded his diamond sword into Mr. Anarchy's side.

"There must have been a glitch, because none of the other people came back," Mr. Anarchy said as he struck Nicholas with his sword.

"Or I'm smart enough to zap myself back on the server. Did you ever think of that?" Nicholas sneered.

"Impossible," Mr. Anarchy retorted, but he wasn't sure he was correct. Maybe Nicholas had the power to zap himself on the server? He wasn't sure.

Lily leapt at Nicholas. "Leave us alone."

"Never," Nicholas shouted. "This battle has just begun."

Lily and Mr. Anarchy were able to weaken Nicholas with blows from their diamond swords. The others splashed potions of harming on him. When two creepers silently lurked behind him, he was destroyed in the explosion.

"We have to find the command blocks before Nicholas respawns." Michael searched the grassy path looking for the abandoned mineshaft.

"How did he get back on the server?" Mr. Anarchy's thoughts were elsewhere; he couldn't focus on finding command blocks if he wasn't sure he even had the power to zap people off the server.

"I'm assuming it was a glitch, if we see the orange and blue griefers," Lily said.

"Or Pablo, Ronan, and Matthew," Simon added. "Then we'll know the lightning bolt isn't working."

"Maybe Nicholas knows how to zap himself onto the server," Lily theorized. "I'm sure most of the other people who left this server would never try to get back on. Maybe it's easier than we think."

"That's a possibility," Mr. Anarchy said.

Benji called out, "I found the mineshaft."

The others raced toward the mineshaft, but an army of creepers flooded the narrow jungle path and exploded. Lily was instantly destroyed. She respawned in her bed, and looked over for Robin.

Seconds later, Robin respawned. "I'm sure Nicholas summoned that creeper invasion."

Lily asked, "Could you believe Nicholas actually wanted to come back on this server? It's so hard to imagine. I can't wait to get back home," Lily said as she put on her armor.

"I know," Robin agreed. "I think we should TP back to the jungle. I also think we have to stop worrying about Nicholas. I'd rather get back to the real world. I want Mr. Anarchy to work his magic with the command blocks."

"Yes," Lily said. "Also, when I get back to the real world, I am going to stay far away from this server."

The two TPed back to the jungle and found everyone was already there. As they stood by the entrance to the mineshaft, Simon called out, "We've been waiting for you."

"We came as quickly as we could," Lily replied.

Mr. Anarchy and Benji were the first to enter the mineshaft. Lily could hear Mr. Anarchy exclaim, "Found it!"

Benji shouted, "Watch out!"

"Help!" Mr. Anarchy yelped. "This mineshaft is filled with spiders!"

The gang sprang into action, clutching their diamond swords tightly, and striking the numerous red-eyed spiders, destroying them.

Michael paused. "I bet there's a spawner in here."

"We have to look for it," suggested Simon.

The two set off deep into the mineshaft to search for the spider spawner. Lily went over to Mr. Anarchy. "Let's get off this server right now. Who cares about Nicholas?"

"I agree, but it takes me a while to summon that bolt." Mr. Anarchy stood by the command blocks.

Michael and Simon came back. Simon announced proudly, "We destroyed the spider spawner."

"Great." Lily smiled.

Robin walked over to the command blocks. "There are so many command blocks. This is fantastic."

Michael counted the enormous stack of command blocks. "One, two, three . . ." he paused. "There must be more than fifty command blocks in this pile."

Simon joked, "You were never that good at math. There are a lot more than fifty command blocks."

"This means we can all go home," Robin cried tears of joy. "I just want to see my friends again."

"I know!" Lily exclaimed. "Finally." Lily didn't express how sad it would be not to share a house with Robin. Also, she'd have to go back to the real world and start waking up for school and helping take out the recycling and her other chores that her parents asked her to do. In Lisimi Village, she didn't have to make her own bed, like she did at home.

Everyone must have had similar thoughts because Simon said, "I bet our old lives are going to seem super boring after living on this server."

"I know," Mr. Anarchy agreed. "Maybe that's why Nicholas zapped himself back onto the server?"

Lily realized Mr. Anarchy was beginning to believe Nicholas didn't return to the server because of a glitch or an error that Mr. Anarchy had made, but that it was a choice. It was a strange choice, but they were all beginning to understand why someone would choose to zap themselves back on the server.

"Should you work on the command blocks here or should we take them back to the village?" asked Michael.

Mr. Anarchy was about to reply, when Nicholas appeared in the mineshaft. "These are my command blocks and you're not taking them anywhere!"

13
IT TAKES A VILLAGE

Ilana and Warren leapt at Nicholas, but they were both destroyed when a second army of creepers quietly snuck into the mineshaft and exploded.

Lily and Robin respawned in the cottage and were about to TP back to the jungle when a loud roar shook the small cottage.

"He spawned the Ender Dragon!" Lily was annoyed.

"Forget about battling the Ender Dragon; we have to go back to the jungle and get those command blocks. I want to go home," Robin said.

"I know." Lily was interrupted when the Ender Dragon's wing struck the side of her house, creating a gaping hole. Rain filled the hole.

"It's raining, too!" Robin exclaimed. "This battle will be trickier than we thought."

Lily was able to plunge her sword into the dragon's wing. It roared and then banged against the house, knocking down an entire wall.

"My cottage!" Lily cried.

"It doesn't matter," Robin reminded her. "We'll be back in the real world soon."

The dragon's side was exposed as it broke down another wall. Lily and Robin were able to strike it with their swords. The dragon lost hearts.

Michael and Simon rushed to the cottage and aimed their bows at the dragon. "Got it!" Simon exclaimed when three of his arrows landed in the dragon.

"It's almost destroyed," Michael called out as a barrage of arrows hit the powerful flying beast.

"I have potions!" Ilana hurried toward them, but two arrows from skeletons that spawned in the rain struck her. Ilana turned around and splashed the potions on the bony beasts.

"Has anyone seen Nicholas?" Mr. Anarchy rushed to his friends.

Sunny, Blossom, Benji, and Warren hurried over.

Sunny called out, "We have!"

Benji added, "We can't leave the jungle mineshaft unattended."

Sunny and Blossom ran toward the Ender Dragon and bravely slammed their swords into the beast, destroying it.

The Ender Dragon dropped an egg, and a portal to the End appeared, but nobody hopped on. They weren't playing the game; they were trying to end the game.

"Let's get back to the jungle," Mr. Anarchy said, as four vacant-eyed zombies lunged at him.

Ilana splashed a potion on the zombies. She spotted Juan and called to him, "Juan, watch out. There are zombies over here. If one of them attacks you, you'll become a zombie villager."

"That's why I'm here," Juan cried out. "Emily is a zombie villager."

Lily and Robin raced over to Juan.

Lily said, "We'll help her."

"I have a golden apple," Robin told them as she grabbed one from her inventory. "I can turn her back into a villager."

The duo rushed to Emily's house, armed with all of the ingredients to change Emily back into a regular villager.

"She's here." Juan pointed to a vacant-eyed Emily strolling through the village streets in a trance-like state.

Lily and Robin worked quickly to help Emily turn back into a villager. When it was complete, Emily thanked them, and then warned, "Watch out!"

Four creepers exploded and Lily and Robin were back in the cottage. The holes in the roof and the walls left them vulnerable to the hostile mobs that spawned in the rainstorm. A group of zombies were in the cottage living room. Lily jumped out of bed and splashed the undead mob with a potion.

Robin stood by Lily's side as the two of them battled the zombies.

Without warning, the rain stopped. Lily looked around the cottage. "It's beyond repair!"

"It's okay," Robin reassured her. "We can rebuild if we have to, but let's hope the command blocks are still in the mineshaft and we can be home soon."

Lily smiled, but the smile quickly disappeared when she heard Michael call out, "Nicholas! Stop!"

Nicholas stood in the center of the village. "Don't bother trying to get those command blocks. And I'm going to make sure you never find your way home."

Nicholas held up a few command blocks. "These are the last command blocks, and I have used them to put you all on Hardcore mode. I'm going to destroy you all."

"If you destroy us, who will you torment?" asked Blossom.

Nicholas snickered, "I'll just zap more people onto the server. It's really no big deal."

"No big deal? It's our lives." Lily couldn't believe how callous Nicholas was and how he lacked any empathy.

"You guys are such a nuisance." Nicholas held the command blocks.

Mr. Anarchy caught up with Nicholas and grabbed the command blocks and destroyed them.

Nicholas hit him with his diamond sword, but Mr. Anarchy splashed a potion of invisibility on himself and disappeared.

"I'm going to get him!" Nicholas screamed.

Sunny and Blossom struck Nicholas until he was destroyed.

14
HIDING SPOTS

"What happened to Mr. Anarchy?" Sunny asked.

"I bet I know where Mr. Anarchy is," said Lily.

"Me too." Robin smiled and looked at the others. "We have to TP to the jungle and find him."

The gang TPed into the heart of the jungle as Benji called out, "I see him!"

"Oh no!" Lily cried while running toward Nicholas.

Nicholas turned around and Lily sliced his hand with her diamond sword. She could hear him moan.

Robin ran to Lily, plunging her sword into Nicholas's side.

Mr. Anarchy screamed, "Over here! The command blocks are still here."

"You're a liar," Lily uttered as she struck Nicholas until he was almost out of hearts.

The gang rushed toward Mr. Anarchy. Ilana asked, "Can you zap us now before Nicholas is destroyed?"

"I think Nicholas should be the first to go. I want to experiment on him. I have to make sure we aren't conducting a fool's errand and we all get back home and get zapped back."

Michael reminded him, "The others didn't come back, so I think we know it will be okay."

Mr. Anarchy was a perfectionist. "I wish I knew a way to make sure you could never get zapped back on again, even if you wanted to."

"Maybe once we are all off the server, we can shut it down," suggested Lily.

"That sounds like a good idea, but I don't know how to do it," admitted Mr. Anarchy.

Nicholas charged toward the group. "You thought I was gone, didn't you?"

Mr. Anarchy whispered to Lily, "Take care of him. I have an idea," and Mr. Anarchy raced toward the stronghold.

Night was beginning to set in. Ilana looked at the sky. "It's going to be a long night."

"I know." Nicholas laughed and splashed a potion of harming on Lily and Ilana.

Lily had an idea. She grabbed bedrock from her inventory, but Nicholas took notice and laughed. "Seriously? You think you're going to trap me in a bedrock room like I did to you and Robin?"

Michael said, "We destroyed that bedrock wall! You're awful."

"I knew you were the one to destroy it!" Lily smiled at Michael as she gathered more supplies to build a makeshift prison for Nicholas.

Six creepers lurked through the dark jungle and crept up behind Lily and Michael. Nicholas didn't warn them. The creepers exploded and Lily was back in Lisimi Village in a cottage that was falling apart. Two skeletons stood over Lily as she respawned in her bed. One of the skeletons stared at Lily as it shot an arrow at her head.

Lily dodged the arrow as Robin respawned in her bed. Robin quickly grabbed her sword and battled the skeletons.

Lily said, "We have to get back to the jungle now. We have to make sure Nicholas is trapped."

"There are so many creepers in the jungle. I lost count," Robin explained. "I think everyone was destroyed."

"What about Mr. Anarchy?" questioned Lily as she destroyed a skeleton.

"I'm not sure," Robin replied. "We have to TP there and find out."

15

CAPTURED

As Lily and Robin arrived in the jungle, they saw Michael and Simon shouting at Nicholas, "Stop the creeper invasion! We know you're summoning them. We don't want them to return."

"Why should I do that?" Nicholas questioned.

Michael held his sword against Nicholas's chest, and called out to his friends, "Someone go inside the mineshaft and tell Mr. Anarchy to put Nicholas on Hardcore mode. We are going to destroy him."

"No!" Nicholas shook. "Don't do that!"

"We have no choice." Michael pierced Nicholas's arm with the diamond sword.

"Go into the prison." Simon splashed a potion on Nicholas, leaving him with only one heart.

"No!" Nicholas shouted.

Ilana sprinted over. "Mr. Anarchy said it's all set. Nicholas is on Hardcore mode. We can destroy him if we'd like and then we'll never have to be bothered by him again."

Tears filled Nicholas's eyes and he quietly wept as he walked into the small bedrock prison. Michael and Simon constructed another wall. They were about to enclose Nicholas in the bedrock prison when Mr. Anarchy rushed out of the mineshaft. "Don't trap him. I'm ready."

"Ready for what?" Nicholas questioned. He was terrified.

"You'll see," Mr. Anarchy said, not directly answering Nicholas's question.

The dark skies filled with clouds and rain fell on the jungle. Ilana took shelter under a large oak tree.

"Now!" Mr. Anarchy called out. "Bring him here."

Nicholas didn't want to leave the bedrock prison, but Michael and Simon chased him out to where Mr. Anarchy ordered him to stand.

A flash of light almost blinded Michael as a lightning bolt struck Nicholas.

"He's gone! It worked!" Lily exclaimed.

"I had to get Nicholas off first because if I didn't, he'd try to thwart all of our attempts to leave."

"I agree," Lily said.

"He was relentless," Mr. Anarchy spoke but his voice was muffled through the thunder.

Benji came over to Mr. Anarchy as another lightning bolt shot through the dark jungle biome. Benji vanished.

Ilana was about to call out that it wasn't fair; she wanted to leave the server, but she kept her mouth closed. She knew Mr. Anarchy was going to find a way to get them all off the server and it would be fair. It didn't matter if you left the server first or last; it only mattered that you were able to get off the server.

The storm ended and everyone commended Mr. Anarchy. He smiled. "I'm glad that worked. Now we have to figure out a fair way to zap everyone back to the real world. And I should let you know that I am going last. I can't leave unless I know everyone is off this server."

Five green creepers could be seen through a patch of leaves. Lily called out, "We never stopped the creeper invasion."

"I couldn't find out where he was spawning them," confessed Mr. Anarchy.

Ilana didn't see the creeper behind her, as it exploded. More creepers flooded the jungle. Soon everyone was destroyed by a creeper and respawned back in Lisimi Village.

When Lily respawned, she was relieved to see the sun was shining. "Look," Lily called out to Robin, who was getting out of bed. "It's daylight."

"We have to find the others," said Robin. "I can't wait to go home."

As Lily and Robin exited the devastated cottage, Lily gasped when she recognized someone in the distance. "It can't be," she cried.

16
SIGNS

"Pablo?" Lily called out.

"Yes." Pablo rushed to Lily and Robin.

"How did you get back on the server? Was there a glitch?" questioned Robin.

"No," Pablo explained. "I am here as a player. I got onto the server without getting zapped back on."

"How?" asked Lily.

"You mean you're at home?" Robin was jealous. She was also bursting with questions. "Did your parents notice you were gone? Are you back at school? What's the date?"

Pablo was overwhelmed and only replied, "It was as if I never left, but I am changed. I mean the experience made me appreciate my real life. I like to sleep through the night without worrying that a zombie is going to drag me from bed and try to kill me. Or if a griefer is going to blow up my house with TNT or many other crazy things that happen in Minecraft that don't happen in the real world."

"What did you have for dinner?" Lily asked as she took an apple from her inventory and took a bite.

"Do you really want to know?" asked Pablo.

"Maybe not." Lily bit into the apple.

Robin said, "We have to go see Mr. Anarchy. Would you like to come with us?"

Pablo said, "Of course. I want him to know that he did a great job getting me off the server. I want to thank him."

As they walked toward Mr. Anarchy's lab, Lily talked rapidly about returning home; she couldn't conceal her excitement. "The first thing I'm doing when I get home is asking my mom to take me out for pizza."

"Pizza." Robin salivated.

"With pepperoni," Lily added.

"And meatballs." Robin started to imagine a large pizza pie. "That's going to be my first meal, too."

Pablo paused and seemed distracted when he said, "Yeah, pizza is great."

"What's the matter, Pablo?" asked Lily.

"My mom wants to use the computer," explained Pablo.

"Does she know that you're trying to help people trapped on the server?" questioned Robin.

"No," Pablo laughed. "She'd never believe me."

"I guess that makes sense," said Lily.

Robin spotted Mr. Anarchy in the distance and called out to him. He started to see Pablo but then stood speechless as he watched Pablo vanish. He caught up to Lily and Robin.

"What happened? Was that Pablo?" Mr. Anarchy asked.

"Yes," Lily exclaimed. "You won't believe it, but Pablo can enter the server as a regular player."

"He was home," Robin told him.

"Yes, he had to leave because his mom needed to use the computer." Lily almost laughed as she spoke those words. It seemed comical that he could leave the server to let his mom use a computer, when they were trapped on the server.

"That's fantastic." Mr. Anarchy was relieved. "I thought there was a glitch and he got zapped back on the server. This means we can all get off the server. We should start zapping people off today."

"Did we come up with a plan for who will get to go first?" asked Lily.

"We're going to have to do something like draw names from a hat," Mr. Anarchy said. "I don't want to start to debate who will go first. It's a waste of time. Nobody will be happy with the outcome."

Warren came over to his friends. "Was I seeing things or did I really see Pablo?"

"Yes." Lily explained how Pablo found a way to return to the server as a player.

"That's awesome. That means once we get home, we can meet up here and we'll always be able to see Juan the Butcher and the other villagers." Warren was thrilled.

Robin added, "And we can go to Lisimi Land. I love the fun house and the roller coaster."

Lily was happy about the possibility of returning to Lisimi Village, but she was also worried about Nicholas. "I hope Nicholas doesn't discover a way to get back on. I don't want him terrorizing us."

"We can't focus on that now. Let's just get off this server. We can always create a new server and meet up there," Mr. Anarchy reminded her.

Warren suggested, "I will gather all the townspeople. We will have one last feast with Juan, Emily, and Fred, and then we'll zap back to the real world."

"Yes, a farewell party!" exclaimed Robin.

Mr. Anarchy said, "Let's all meet by my lab. After the party, I'll start to summon the lightning bolts."

"I'll get everyone together," Warren said and rushed off.

17
THE FIRST ONES

The energy was high in Lisimi Village. Everyone was ready for a party. The gang brought all sorts of treats for the party. Juan cooked savory meats and Fred the Farmer carried potatoes, carrots, and other vegetables. Emily the Fisherwoman spent the morning fishing for the party, and she brought fresh fish.

Lily announced, "Today is the day we all get back home. I also wanted you to know that Pablo returned to the server as a regular player."

Kaboom!

Nobody had time to warn Lily that a horde of creepers was about to explode behind her. Lily respawned in her bed, and sprinted back to Lisimi Village in her armor.

"What happened?" Lily called out.

Only Warren remained in the town. "Everyone was destroyed by creepers. There were hundreds of them in the town."

"Do you think Nicholas is back? Or is it because we never found the spawner?" Lily worried.

"I'm not sure, but we have to figure this out. I want to go home and this creeper invasion isn't going to stop me." Warren was annoyed.

Mr. Anarchy exited his lab and caught up to Lily. "We have to stop this creeper invasion. It's going to interfere with our plan."

"How can we stop the invasion?" Lily asked.

Pablo came back on the server. "What's wrong? Can I help you guys?"

"I think Nicholas must have left a creeper spawner or has a hostile mob farm in that mineshaft. We have to stop it before we zap everyone off the server," Mr. Anarchy said.

Pablo shook his head. "I am going to check it out. I can deactivate it for you."

"Thanks." Mr. Anarchy smiled.

The townspeople walked back to the party. Juan the Butcher exclaimed, "Let's forget about the creepers and have a good time. This will be our last feast together."

Lily reminded him, "It might not be our last meal. I think we found a way to get back on the server."

Juan said, "Well, this is our last real meal. Soon you'll be able to eat much better food."

The gang dined on mooshroom stew, chicken, carrots, potatoes, and drank milk. Everyone took their best food from their inventory, offering it to their friends. After eating two pieces of cake, Lily confessed that she was full. "I don't want to leave the server with a stomachache."

Robin looked at the sky. "It's almost nighttime; we have to summon the lightning soon."

Mr. Anarchy reminded everyone, "We can't do it until Pablo deactivates the creeper spawner."

Ilana suggested, "Maybe we should figure out who will be the first person to get zapped off. We don't have time to waste."

Warren said, "We have to put papers on the ground with names on them, and I'll pick one up and announce who it is."

Everyone agreed that was the best plan.

As everyone placed the names on the ground, Pablo TPed back to Lisimi Village, announcing, "It's destroyed. You won't be attacked by any more creepers. And I also found a few treasure chests filled with diamonds and gold. You guys should really go on a treasure hunt before you leave."

Ilana gasped. "No way! I just want to go home. I couldn't care less about treasure."

Robin repeated, "It's almost nighttime. We have to get started."

Warren picked the first name from the ground and read it aloud, "Ilana."

Ilana beamed. "This is the best news ever."

Mr. Anarchy walked into his lab and used the command blocks to summon the lightning bolt. The sky grew cloudy and a lightning bolt shot through the sky, striking Ilana.

Ilana disappeared.

"It worked!" Lily called out to Mr. Anarchy.

"Who's next?" Michael asked.

18
HOPE

Warren picked up another name from the ground. "Sunny."

Sunny waited for the lightning bolt. Blossom raced to his side. "See you in the real world, Sunny."

Sunny smiled. The lightning bolt struck him and he was zapped off the server. Blossom wept.

"Can I go next?" she pleaded.

Warren said, "We have to pick the names from the ground. It's the only way. I'm sorry."

Blossom's sobs grew louder.

Lily walked over to Blossom. "You never know; your name might be the next one called."

Warren picked up another name. "Peter."

Peter asked, "Can I trade and let Blossom use my turn?"

"That's very nice of you, but we can't do that. We have to follow these rules. It has to be fair and orderly," Warren replied sternly.

Before Peter could protest, he was struck by the lightning and Peter was removed from the server.

Blossom stood next to Warren, looking at his hand as he grabbed another name. "Blossom."

Blossom cheered. "Thanks, and I'll miss you all!"

Blossom rushed toward the lightning, instantly vanishing.

Lily was waiting for her name to be called when Peter spawned in front of her.

"Are you really here or are you a player?" asked Lily.

Peter stood frozen, his eyes filled with tears.

Pablo said, "He's back. I can tell who is a player and who is stuck in the server."

"Peter," Warren shrieked. "What happened?"

Peter whimpered, "Ask Mr. Anarchy. I have no idea."

Mr. Anarchy sprinted from the lab. "Peter, I'm sorry. There is something wrong with the command blocks. There is a glitch."

Blossom respawned in the center of the village. "What?" she hollered.

"There's a glitch," Mr. Anarchy apologized.

Pablo remarked, "You were able to get Ilana and Sunny off of the server, and I know you'll be able to get everyone off soon."

"Thanks, Pablo, I just have to work on the command blocks." Mr. Anarchy had to experiment with the command blocks to figure out why there was a glitch.

Robin pointed to the sky. "It's getting dark. We have to get inside or we'll be attacked by hostile mobs."

There was a collective moan; everyone was disappointed they wouldn't be zapped off that night.

"We can't go back to the cottage; it's not safe there. It's missing walls." Lily looked at Robin.

Michael offered, "Stay at my house. I have a lot of room."

Simon added, "I'm staying there. It will be fun."

Lily and Robin followed Michael to his house, as Mr. Anarchy went back to the lab to figure out how he could fix the glitch and get everyone off the server.

Michael smiled. "If this is our last night in Lisimi Village, I'm glad I get to spend it with all of you."

The gang hurried toward Michael's house, escaping any hostile mobs that might be spawning in the dark. As they entered the house, they quickly climbed into bed. Lily looked over at her friends. "Good night. Tomorrow, we might be in our real beds."

Robin wished them all sweet dreams.

Lily dreamt about being in her home and waking up to have breakfast with her family. She knew this was one dream that was definitely going to come true.

READ ON FOR AN EXCITING SNEAK PEEK AT THE FINAL BOOK IN

Winter Morgan's
Unofficial Minetrapped Adventure series

1
TRY AGAIN

"I see it!" Simon called out.

"Great," Lily exclaimed. "Can you reach it?"

Michael looked at Simon and grabbed a pickaxe. "We'll have to mine to get it," he said.

Lily picked up her pickaxe and banged it against the blocky ground. "I see it too!"

The gang dug deep into the floor of the mine until Lily, Simon, and Michael were surrounded by blue.

Lily cried out, "Diamonds!"

"Sweet!" Michael exclaimed, and he grabbed as many diamonds as he could fit in his hands.

"This is the best mining job ever," Simon declared as he stuffed his inventory with diamonds.

"We should trade these at the blacksmith's shop and get more armor," Lily suggested.

"Good idea," Simon agreed as he scanned the mine. "I think we have all of them. Let's go back to Lisimi Village."

Blossom hurried into the mine. "Guess what, guys?"

"What is it, Blossom?" asked Lily.

"I think Mr. Anarchy has figured out the glitch. There are people crowded outside his lab." Blossom beamed.

"Wow," Simon exclaimed. "That's fantastic news."

"Is it true? How can we be sure? Maybe there is another reason people are at Mr. Anarchy's lab." Michael spit out a slew of questions. He was skeptical.

It had been a while since Sunny and the others were zapped off the server. Mr. Anarchy had come close to discovering why there was a glitch, but none of his attempts to solve it were successful, and Michael had been disappointed way too many times.

"I think this is it. I think it's real," Blossom told him.

"I hope so," Michael replied as he followed Blossom and the others back to Lisimi Village.

Simon remarked, "I've really enjoyed these last few months in Lisimi Village. It's a lot of fun to stay on this server when we aren't battling griefers."

The past few months had been peaceful, and the gang was able to explore the server. They had traveled to various biomes. One day they had an enormous snowball fight in the icy cold biome with all of the townspeople.

"Remember the snowball fight?" Lily recalled with a chuckle.

"I still have an inventory full of snowballs," Blossom gloated. "While you guys were busy pounding each other with frozen snowballs, I was collecting them."

"Why did you bother? It's not like anyone is going to spawn Nether mobs in the Overworld," Simon said. "We don't have any griefers to battle."

"You never know." Blossom defended her reasoning for hoarding snowballs, "I can use them when I'm in the Nether searching for treasure."

As the gang entered the village, Emily the Fisherwoman and Juan the Butcher approached them. Juan called out, "I think Mr. Anarchy has an announcement."

"We know!" Blossom replied, "I hope it's good news!"

"I think it is," Emily said. "I'm pretty sure he's found a way to get you guys back to the real world. There is a line forming outside his lab."

"Hope so!" Michael exclaimed. He was finally hopeful this would be the day he could go home.

Juan admitted, "I'll miss you guys."

"We'll try to come and visit like Pablo did," Lily told him, "but we'll miss you too. It's going to be hard trying to readjust to our old lives."

"You'll do fine," Emily said with a smile. "Go ahead and find out. Let us know."

The gang headed for Mr. Anarchy's lab. Although Lily had heard there was a long line outside his lab, she was still shocked when she saw it with her own eyes.

"Wow," Lily exclaimed, "look at how many people are waiting. It will take forever for everyone to get off the server."

"But we'll get off okay. I just know it," Blossom proclaimed.

Michael walked over to a townsperson standing on line and asked, "Is it true? Has Mr. Anarchy finally found a way to get us all home?"

The townsperson shrugged. "I'm not sure. Peter said Mr. Anarchy had a big announcement. Everyone raced over and once we got here, Peter told us to line up."

"Where is Peter?" Michael asked. He didn't see him on the line.

"I don't know. Nobody has seen Peter or Mr. Anarchy for a while. We've all been just standing on this line waiting."

"Really?" Michael began to worry.

Lily stood next to Michael and said, "I'm going to get some answers. I can't just stand here and wait." She entered the lab and called out, "Mr. Anarchy?"

There was no response.

Lily called out again, "Mr. Anarchy? Where are you?"

"In here." His voice was very faint.

Lily walked down a long dimly lit corridor. A pair of red eyes glared at her. She grabbed her diamond sword and struck the spider before it could inject her with any of its poison.

"Lily," Mr. Anarchy said as he ran toward her. "There you are. I'm having a bit of a problem."

"What happened?" asked Lily.

"I thought I found a way to get everyone off the server, but then I realized that it might not work. There is a line of people in front of my lab, and I don't want to disappoint them. I'm not sure how to let them know I made a mistake," confessed Mr. Anarchy.

"I knew it wouldn't work," a voice called out from behind them.

Lily turned around to see Michael approaching and she tried to explain his words to Mr. Anarchy. "Michael has been very sad lately. He keeps getting his hopes up and gets very upset when he's disappointed."

"I don't blame him," Mr. Anarchy said. "I'm upset with myself. I should have found a solution by now. I work tirelessly day and night, but I can't come up with any answers. It feels so pointless."

"No, it's not." Lily knew she had to give Mr. Anarchy a pep talk, but she didn't want to tell him to try harder because she knew he was trying as hard as he could. "You're doing your best. I know you feel it's impossible to solve this problem, but I have faith that you'll find a way to crack this code."

Mr. Anarchy smiled in appreciation. "You always make me feel better."

Lily continued to offer her support to Mr. Anarchy. "Maybe if you tell me what you're doing I can help."

"Okay." Mr. Anarchy rattled off the various ways he had worked with the command blocks to get everyone out of Lisimi Village and back to the real world.

Lily stood by the command blocks, listening to Mr. Anarchy's many stories about his failed experiments. Suddenly, they both heard a loud roar.

"What is that?" Lily gasped.

A scaly wing crashed into the lab and Mr. Anarchy leapt back, shielding himself from the rubble. "Oh no! It's the Ender Dragon!"